...of Justice. ...ter walls, and even freeze crooks in crystal – and it always returns to J. B.'s hand

Thirty/Thirty transforms from a large horse to a huge Humanoid robot with a lever action freeze gun to help BraveStarr

Handle Bar runs the trading post on New Texas. He weighs over fourteen tons, and no one has ever been known to injure him

Deputy Fuzz – Marshal BraveStarr's 'go-between' with the Prairie People who live in underground burrows on New Texas

Light years from Earth, in a distant galaxy, is the planet of New Texas. It had nothing that anyone wanted until suddenly, kerium crystals were discovered there. Kerium is both rare and valuable — it is used to power Earth's spaceships!

So New Texas became important. First came prospectors, then came ordinary citizens, both good and bad. Most however were bad, and the planet needed some lawmen. The Galactic Council sent just one — Marshal BraveStarr. It turned out he was enough.

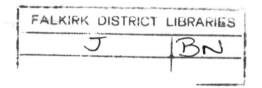

British Library Cataloguing in Publication Data
Alexander, Ian
    The phantom herd.—(Marshal BraveStarr; 1).
    I. Title   II. Davies, Robin, *1950-*   III. Series
    823′.914[J]   PZ7
    ISBN 0-7214-1036-7

First edition

Published by Ladybird Books Ltd Loughborough Leicestershire UK
Ladybird Books Inc Lewiston Maine 04240 USA

BRAVESTARR © MCMLXXXVII FILMATION ASSOCIATES All rights reserved
BraveStarr ® and associated characters are trademarks of Filmation Associates

© MCMLXXXVII LADYBIRD BOOKS LTD in text and presentation

Printed in England

FILMATION'S

BRAVESTARR ®

The
Phantom Herd

by Ian Alexander

illustrated by Robin Davies

Ladybird Books

Marshal BraveStarr and the Phantom Herd

Marshal BraveStarr had been away on vacation. The chief lawman of that unruly planet, New Texas, had enjoyed his well-deserved break. When the kerium shuttle landed at the Spacedrome in the desert outside Fort Kerium, he was surprised that nobody was there to meet him. He felt sure that his faithful Equestroid Thirty/Thirty would have come out to fetch him.

It is quite a long way into Fort Kerium, so he

decided to hire a Turbo-Mule from Mavis Self-Drive.
The rented robot tried to sink its titanium teeth into
his knee as he mounted! Turbo-Mules are
programmed to be User-Friendly but it takes a crafty
robot to catch our hero off his guard. He used his
Speed of Puma to dodge the bite, and a touch of his
Strength of Bear soon had it heading townwards.

Then, as he rode towards Fort Kerium, he was puzzled by the billowing dust cloud over the town. There are dust storms in plenty on that desert planet, but somehow this did not look natural. He knew that just before he'd gone away, the town engineers had been fitting the Fort with a new type of ground-effect lifter like a hovercraft.

The idea was that the town could take off on air jets. Then the citizens could move it whenever they felt like a change of view. From the way the dust was pulsing up into the sky, it looked as though someone was switching the lifter on and off, making the whole town leap up and down. Curiouser and curiouser!

Shortly, he came to the town's name board. Normally, this gives a digital read-out of the number of people in town. But now it seemed that the electronic link had broken, and the board was being kept up to date by his trusty Deputy, Fuzz.

Hot, bothered and hat-less, Deputy Fuzz was listening to the sounds of a real ole gun battle going on in town. Fuzz was hard pressed to keep count of the freeze-gun shots. He was chalking up the score in three columns: RUNNIN' LOOSE; FROZE; DEFROSTIN'.

It was a hot day under the desert sun. Fuzz reckoned that even after a full blast from a freeze-gun, they'd only be staying frozen for around five minutes.

BraveStarr asked Fuzz what had happened to Thirty/Thirty. He could not figure out why the mammoth Equestroid had not waded in with his huge lever-action freeze-rifle, which he lovingly called Sara Jane, to stop the riot in the town.

Fuzz reminded him that Thirty/Thirty just loves to try out any new bionic gizmos that will give him even more strength. During the night, someone had left a parcel for Thirty/Thirty on the Jail House doorstep. Fuzz suspected it must have been Tex Hex, leader of the planet's baddies. The package turned out to contain spring-heeled hooves of SuperMetal. Thirty/Thirty had been delighted.

At first he got on very well with them, but he soon became very thirsty, teaching himself to leap over buildings in the heat of the mid-day sun. When he had gone into Handle Bar's Saloon for a sweet water, the place was full of Tex Hex's mob, as usual.

It seemed that one of them had slipped something into his drink to start him hiccuping.

The first of Thirty/Thirty's mighty hiccups had set him bouncing on his springs like a crazy horse. He wrecked Handle Bar's best chandelier as he left through the ceiling. He'd been hiccuping and bouncing ever since. "Look," said Fuzz, pointing through the heat haze at a line of distant dust-puffs spurting from the desert, "thar he goes!"

BraveStarr knew he would have to think of a way to rescue Thirty/Thirty. But first, he had to stop the even bigger bounces of Fort Kerium. If it carried on leaping up and down on its ground-effect machine, the whole town would shake to bits.

He tried to make his hired Turbo-Mule jump aboard the heaving city but it backed off. So he decided to rely on his own powers. By using his Speed of Puma and Strength of Bear, he managed to leap on to the edge of Fort Kerium. As he jumped, the city suddenly returned to desert level, missing him by a whisker.

In the leaping town, the big shoot-out with freeze-guns was still going on. The law abiding locals were fighting it out with the evil allies of Tex Hex, such as Thunderstick, Cactushead, and the Dingomen.

Every minute or so Fort Kerium was pounding down on to the desert floor. Teeth jarred and bits fell off buildings as BraveStarr fought his way through the thick of the shoot-out into the Fort's Control Room.

There he found a burro running in circles trying to get at a carrot tied to its tail. Every time it came round, it tripped the power switch for the ground-effect lifters. He pulled the main plug out and the town came to rest in a final cloud of dust, to lie quiet at last. He gave the burro the carrot.

Only Tex Hex could have been so cruel.

But where *was* Tex? BraveStarr found out from Handle Bar that Tex Hex had left town *before* it had started leaping. It seemed very odd that Tex had left before his mob started the fight. BraveStarr knew that he just loved to be at the centre of any trouble going. In fact, the town had only started jumping just before the Marshal's flight was due in.

Handle Bar had been really puzzled because so many of the Prairie People were missing. He hadn't seen many of them for a week back. But then he had heard tell that Deputy Fuzz had told the Prairie People the Bank had been robbed. The Deputy had called out all the strong ones on a posse and they had ridden off East.

This didn't figure. BraveStarr had just been talking to Fuzz and surely he would have told him about a robbery! Something odd *was* going on.

BraveStarr went down to the Bank. He found it had not been robbed, but the manager was complaining to Judge J. B. He said that because everybody *thought* all the money had been stolen, nobody was coming in. He wanted to sue somebody for his loss of business, but who?

The Judge thought it was all part of Tex Hex's plan. Perhaps all these strange goings-on were a clever plot to fox the Marshal. Maybe the Baddies were up to no good somewhere out of town. That would fit in with keeping Thirty/Thirty bouncing about the desert too. And what about the missing Prairie People? Since the Bank had not been robbed, that posse smelt like a trick as well!

Deputy Fuzz arrived. No, he had certainly not raised a posse. He scratched the fur on top of his head as he tried to figure it all out.

BraveStarr asked when he had lost his Deputy Hat. He said it had vanished a week or more ago. He'd reported it stolen to himself, but what with the Marshal being away, he had been too busy on other things to do any detective work for himself....

So, if it wasn't Fuzz who had called out the fake posse, who was it? Surely it must have been Outlaw Scuzz, the only Prairie Person to have gone to the bad. He and Fuzz look very like each other. People often mix them up. The easiest way to tell them apart is by their hats! Normally, Scuzz wears a Stove-pipe Hat, quite different from Fuzz's Deputy Hat. Judge J. B. worked out that Scuzz must have swapped the Stove-pipe Hat for the stolen Deputy Hat to fool people into thinking he was Fuzz!

She dreamed up a plan for getting their own back. They would play the same trick on Tex Hex's baddies. Why not get a Stove-pipe Hat for Fuzz and let him head East, tracking the posse? He could sneak past Tex Hex's guards by pretending to be Scuzz and get in touch with the Prairie People to find out what was going on.

Fuzz scurried off while BraveStarr set about rescuing Thirty/Thirty from the hiccups. After a long chase across the sandflats on the Turbo-Mule, he tracked down his bucking steed by following the bounce marks. Shaking out his lasso, BraveStarr built his loop and sent it snaking skywards.

It jerked tight around the lurching Equestroid glinting far overhead in the desert sun. BraveStarr swarmed up the rope with Strength of Bear. With Speed of Puma, he unstrapped the springs. Thirty/Thirty hit the sand with a breath-stopping thump. He was dazed and sore but free of the hiccups at last!

Soon they were on their way, BraveStarr riding
Thirty/Thirty and Judge J. B. on her Turbo-Stallion.
She was armed with her Hammer of Justice and she
took one of her travelling Copterclinks for hauling
the crooks off to Fort Kerium jail. They tracked the
posse-prints through the desert, speeded on their
way by following Fuzz's clues. He had left marks on
the cactus, blazing the trail.

Fuzz, a day ahead of them, came to the edge of a canyon. A great sheet of rock hung over the rim, topped by a line of teetering rock pinnacles. In the cliff face he could see the mouths of tunnels.

He jammed his Stove-pipe Hat disguise firmly on his head. It was getting dark and, despite his knocking knees, he fooled Tex Hex's sentries. They didn't give him a second glance, never doubting that he was Scuzz.

In the tunnels he found the captive Prairie People who had been lured away on the false posse. Some of them were being forced to dig into the canyon wall. Tex's mob were making them dig out fossil bones, buried deep in the rocks that made up the side of the canyon.

Beyond the tunnels, Fuzz found a huge cave.
Here more of the Prairie People prisoners were being
made to fit together the fossil bones and bring them
back to life with bionics. They were turning out rows
of robot Longhornosaurs. Dingomen herders were
driving them up to the top of the canyon and
parking them as a great Phantom Herd on land above
the cliff. There is no grazing in the desert now but
Tex Hex had powered them with solar cells. There
they could soak in the sunlight during the long days.

Fuzz heard from the captive Prairie People that
Tex's plan was to make himself overlord of the

planet. His huge herd of mindless monsters would be made to stampede to order. The horde of Longhornosaurs would obey his commands and trample into the dust anybody who got in his way.

Fuzz pretended to be nasty to his friends. The Dingomen laughed, sure he was Scuzz, so he had no trouble passing the guards again. Soon he was out in the desert night, wondering how to find the Marshal. That was no problem either. BraveStarr was listening out for him coming with his Ears of Wolf and soon spotted him in the gloom by using his Eyes of Hawk.

Fuzz was feeling quite a hero. He said he would go back and bluff his way through the enemy sentries yet again so that he could lead a dawn breakout of the captive Prairie People. This time the Stove-pipe Hat would serve not only as a disguise but as his means of smuggling in the Judge's Hammer of Justice! He would use it to blast a hole through the roof of the tunnel (which was in rock too hard for burrowing).

Meanwhile, BraveStarr and Thirty/Thirty had another job to do, above ground. But they couldn't start until there was daylight. That was why Fuzz was going to wait until morning before freeing his people. BraveStarr and Thirty/Thirty clambered up on top of a rock outcrop and made themselves comfortable in the moon shadows. Up there, they could see without being seen. They spent the long hours listening to the howling and yodelling of the Dingomen night herders who worked for Tex Hex.

At last, dawn came. Thirty/Thirty fired Sara Jane into the air, and even deep underground Fuzz heard her mighty voice. That was the signal for him to raise his hat and produce J. B.'s Hammer, to reply by blasting a hole in the roof of the prison tunnel.

As the Prairie People streamed out of the hole, BraveStarr leapt into Thirty/Thirty's saddle and started a sunrise stampede of his own. He planned to confuse the guards and help the escapers, but his main aim was to get rid of the menace of the Phantom Fossil Herd.

As our heroes got the Longhornosaurs up and running, Tex Hex started an attack of his own to try to frighten BraveStarr off. Hex's men fired at him every time his head showed above the plunging backs of the beasts. BraveStarr tried to dodge their freeze-gun blasts by hanging half out of the saddle. Using his Neutra-Laser, he fired back at them from under Thirty/Thirty's neck. In the hassle and dust he knew he couldn't shoot straight. He aimed to make *them* keep their heads down and let him get the robots turned towards the lip of the canyon.

Just as the sun came up as a crimson ball on the desert rim, BraveStarr succeeded in turning the stampede. The robots of the Phantom Herd went trundling blindly over the edge of the cliff into the lilac-shadowed depths of the canyon.

BraveStarr vaulted out of Thirty/Thirty's saddle. It was time for the Equestroid to transform himself into his towering eight-foot Humanoid mode. Thirty/Thirty did not have to be told what to do. He fired Sara Jane, his enormous freeze-cannon. He made the whole cliff top come crashing down onto the Phantom Herd.

The Longhornosaur bones were re-fossilised (for the time being at least...) and the planet was saved.

The sudden eerie silence was broken by drumming hoof beats. Tex Hex, not well pleased, was high-tailing off to his stronghold in the Hexagon.

In a last flurry of action, the Marshal arrested Scuzz and popped him into J. B.'s Copterclink.

Marshal BraveStarr yawned and thumbed his Stetson back on his forehead. He thought to himself that sometimes vacations seem more trouble than they are worth. He hadn't had any sleep since he got back to New Texas. He hoped that the engineers had finished taking apart the ground-effect lifter. As soon as he reached home he was going to have a good snooze, and he certainly didn't want to be tossed out of bed by a leaping town...

Vipra is a cold blooded snake lady who sometimes works for Tex Hex, but prefers to work on her own

Thunderstick is a bad tempered robot who is one of Tex Hex's toughest allies

Sandstorm is a sand walrus. He can blow a fine mist from his mouth that puts people to sleep

Outlaw Scuzz is dirty and shabby, and is the only Prairie Person who has ever turned bad. He goes in for nasty practical jokes